ANCIENT GREEK M

TROJAN
HORSE

Author
Gilly Cameron Cooper

Consultant
Nick Saunders

Copyright © ticktock Entertainment Ltd 2007
First published in Great Britain in 2007 by ticktock Media Ltd.,
Unit 2, Orchard Business Centre, North Farm Road,
Tunbridge Wells, Kent, TN2 3XF

ticktock project editor: Jo Hanks
ticktock project designer: Graham Rich

We would like to thank: Indexing Specialists (UK) Ltd.

ISBN 978 1 84696 064 2
Printed in China
A CIP catalogue record for this book is available from the British Library.

CONTENTS

THE GREEKS, THEIR GODS & MYTHS

The ancient Greeks lived in a world dominated by the Mediterranean Sea, the snow-capped mountains that surrounded it, dangerous winds, and sudden storms. They saw their lives as controlled by the gods and spirits of Nature, and told myths about how the gods fought with each other and created the universe. It was a world of chance and luck, of magic and superstition, in which the endless myths made sense of a dangerous and unpredictable life.

The ancient Greek gods looked and acted like human beings. They fell in love, were jealous, vain, and argued with each other. Unlike humans, they were immortal. This meant they did not die, but lived forever. They also had superhuman strength and magical powers. Each god had a power that belonged only to them.

In the myths, the gods sometimes had children with humans. These children were born demi-gods and might have special powers, but were usually mortal and could die. When their human children were in trouble, the Olympian gods would help them.

The gods liked to meddle in to human life. Different gods took sides with different people. The gods also liked to play tricks on humans. They did

this for all sorts of reasons: because it was fun; because they would gain something; and also for revenge. The Ancient Greeks believed that 12 Olympian gods ruled over the world at any time. The 10 gods and goddesses that you see here were always Olympians, they were the most important ones. Some of them you'll meet in our story.

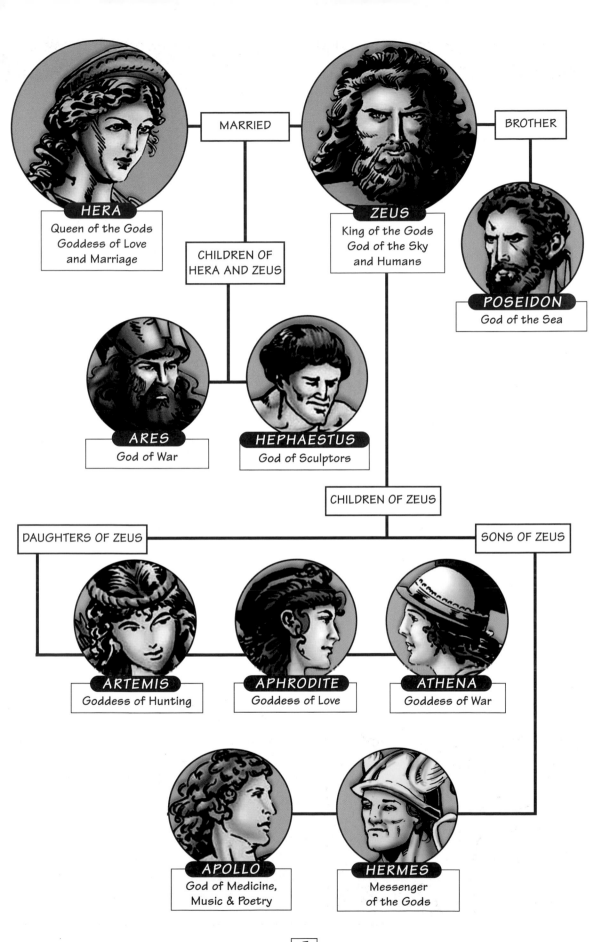

HERA
Queen of the Gods
Goddess of Love
and Marriage

MARRIED

ZEUS
King of the Gods
God of the Sky
and Humans

BROTHER

POSEIDON
God of the Sea

CHILDREN OF
HERA AND ZEUS

ARES
God of War

HEPHAESTUS
God of Sculptors

CHILDREN OF ZEUS

DAUGHTERS OF ZEUS

SONS OF ZEUS

ARTEMIS
Goddess of Hunting

APHRODITE
Goddess of Love

ATHENA
Goddess of War

APOLLO
God of Medicine,
Music & Poetry

HERMES
Messenger
of the Gods

SETTING THE SCENE

Some 3,260 years ago Greece was not one big united country. It was made up of lots of small kingdoms called city-states, such as Athens, Sparta and Mycenae. Each city-state had its own leader. The most powerful was Agamemnon, King of Mycenae. The Myceneans controlled some of the most important trade routes in the Mediterranean Sea. Because of this they had power over other tribes and city-states throughout Greece. If Agamemnon ordered other tribes to fight for him, they had no choice. The Trojans were different because they were a wealthy nation in their own right. They controlled many important trade routes from their great city, Troy. There had been jealousy between the Trojans and Mycenean Greeks for many years before our story starts.

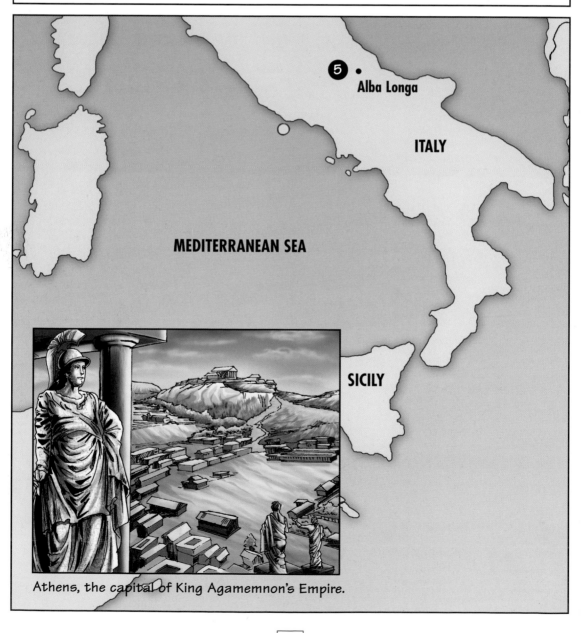

Athens, the capital of King Agamemnon's Empire.

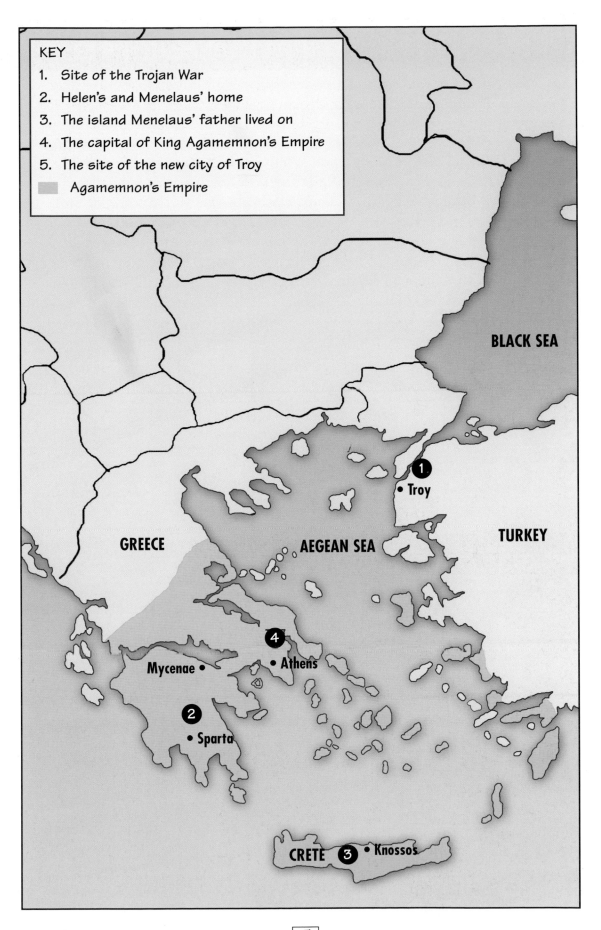

KEY

1. Site of the Trojan War
2. Helen's and Menelaus' home
3. The island Menelaus' father lived on
4. The capital of King Agamemnon's Empire
5. The site of the new city of Troy

   Agamemnon's Empire

BLACK SEA

1 • Troy

GREECE

AEGEAN SEA

TURKEY

4
Mycenae •   • Athens

2
• Sparta

CRETE **3** • Knossos

BEWARE THE WRATH OF THE GODS

Hecuba, wife of King Priam of Troy was pregnant. One night, she saw a blazing city in her dreams. An Oracle told her: "This is a terrible sign. The child in your womb will ruin Troy. You must kill it!". When the baby was born, Priam gave it to his chief herdsman, Agelaus. The herdsman left the baby to die on Mount Ida, a hill overlooking Troy. When Agelaus returned a few days later, he found the baby alive and healthy because it had been kept alive by a wild bear. Agelaus saw this as a sign that the child was meant to live. He decided to look after it. He called the baby Paris, and the lad grew up to be clever, strong and very good-looking. He helped Agelaus look after his flocks. All this time, Paris had no idea that he was a prince of Troy.

Agelaus, you must kill this child.

Poor little thing!

Paris' good looks and bravery caught the attention of the gods. At the same time, the mighty Zeus decided he was tired of hearing his wife, Hera, arguing with the goddesses Athena and Aphrodite. They were fighting over which one of them was the most beautiful.

Hmm, if Paris is as clever as he is good-looking, he can decide who is the most beautiful goddess.

8

One day, the three goddesses visited Paris while he was herding his goats. "Zeus says you have to give this golden apple to whoever you think is the most beautiful of us", they announced. Paris wondered how he, an ordinary man, could possibly judge. One by one, the goddesses approached Paris. Each offered him a wonderful prize if he chose them. Hera went first.

Choose me, I'll make you lord of Asia and the richest man in the world.

Athena was next.

Choose me and you will be victorious in battle, and the wisest, most handsome man in the world.

Choose me and I'll give you the love of Helen, the most beautiful woman who has ever lived.

Paris couldn't say no to Aphrodite's prize. In doing so, he fatally upset the other two. Muttering angrily, they hatched a nasty plot.

Hera, we will make him pay for this!

The most beautiful woman? Promise? OK, you win the golden apple.

In the meantime, Paris' life went back to normal. Until one day, he went into Troy to take part in the yearly games. He won the boxing and running events, to the embarrassment of the king's sons. To save the family pride, two of the sons, Hector and Diephobus, challenged Paris to a fight. Agelaus was terrified that Paris would be killed and rushed towards King Priam.

Save him, King Priam, he is your son!

Paris was spared death and welcomed back as the long-lost prince.

Paris couldn't stop thinking of Helen. He knew the famous beauty lived in Sparta and soon found an excuse to visit her. The Trojan prince was welcomed in Sparta as an honoured guest. Unfortunately Helen had a husband, King Menelaus. The king was suddenly called away to his father's funeral in Crete. With the coast clear, Aphrodite began to work her magic on Paris and Helen.

Come back to Troy with me, Helen.

Hera, have mercy on me. I'm so in love, I'll have to go.

The night Menelaus left, Paris and Helen ran away together.

What have we done? May Aphrodite protect us!

Don't be frightened. My people will love you.

Menelaus was very angry. He stormed off to his brother Agamemnon, the most powerful king in Greece, to ask for his help.

Help me raise an army. This is an insult to us and the whole of Greece.

Hmmm, it is a good chance to add Troy to my empire.

Helen's beauty charmed the Trojans. King Priam swore never to let her go. But one day, Helen was gazing out to sea when she saw ships in the distance. She knew at once Menelaus had come to get her back. And he'd brought armies from all over Agememnon's empire.

What have I done? This face of mine has launched a thousand deadly ships against Troy.

DEADLOCK

Ten years had passed since Helen first saw the horizon fill with Greek ships. For nine years the Greeks camped outside the walls holding the city under siege. Many a bloody skirmish, duel and battle was fought on the windy plains outside the walls, with no decisive victory. Brave warriors from both sides were killed. They knew that the only way to beat the Trojans once and for all was to get over the city walls, but that seemed impossible.

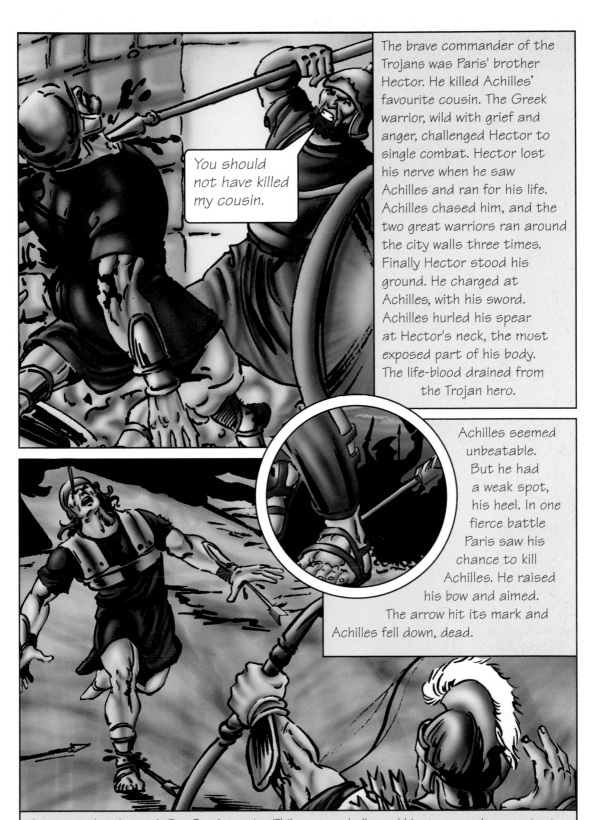

You should not have killed my cousin.

The brave commander of the Trojans was Paris' brother Hector. He killed Achilles' favourite cousin. The Greek warrior, wild with grief and anger, challenged Hector to single combat. Hector lost his nerve when he saw Achilles and ran for his life. Achilles chased him, and the two great warriors ran around the city walls three times. Finally Hector stood his ground. He charged at Achilles, with his sword. Achilles hurled his spear at Hector's neck, the most exposed part of his body. The life-blood drained from the Trojan hero.

Achilles seemed unbeatable. But he had a weak spot, his heel. In one fierce battle Paris saw his chance to kill Achilles. He raised his bow and aimed. The arrow hit its mark and Achilles fell down, dead.

Paris was also doomed. The Greek warrior Philoctetes challenged him to an archery contest... to the death. Paris didn't stand a chance. Though the first arrow went wide, the second pierced his hand and the third blinded his right eye. But it was the fourth, which pierced Paris' ankle, that wounded him mortally. After his death, Helen was forced to marry Deiphobus, one of Paris' brothers. Still the battle raged on between the Greeks and the Trojans.

The Greeks knew that the only way to beat the Trojans was to break through the massive walls that went around the city. But so far they hadn't been able to.

The gods were also tired seeing so many people dying. Zeus held a council, and suggested the gods let Menelaus take Helen home without any more bloodshed. But Athena still wanted revenge, because Paris hadn't chosen her as the most beautiful goddess. Athena looked down on the Greeks wondering what she could do to finish the war. Her eyes fell on Epeius, a carpenter. He was carving animals, which gave her an idea...

Athena gave Epeius step-by-step instructions. First, she told Epeius to gather logs from the forest around the plain. Day after day, he cut down trees and made planks.

The Greek soldiers watched in amazement as a massive frame rose high above the camp. Then, Epeius laid planks over the framework and pegged them in place.

Epeius and Athena finally finished their project. It was a giant wooden horse. High up, underneath it, a trapdoor swung open to reveal a hollow belly, like an enormous cave.

One man knew exactly what it was for. He was Odysseus, a crafty Greek who had been given instructions by Athena. Odysseus handpicked a group of the bravest Greek warriors. The group included Menelaus, who wanted to find Helen, and Neoptolemus, son of the mighty Achilles.

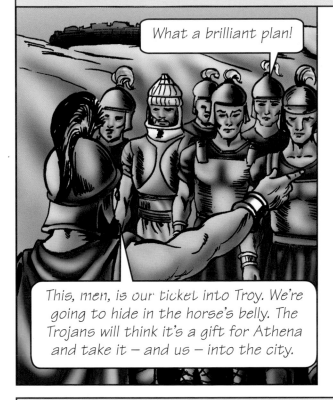

What a brilliant plan!

This, men, is our ticket into Troy. We're going to hide in the horse's belly. The Trojans will think it's a gift for Athena and take it — and us — into the city.

I made it, why do I have to go?

Because, Epeius, you're the only one who knows how to work the trapdoor.

One by one, the warriors climbed into the belly of the horse. Epeius rolled up the ladder and shut the trapdoor. No-one outside could see the door. The warriors sat in darkness, prepared for a long wait.

We stick it out here until the rest pack up camp, and sail off.

If the Trojans guess we're inside, then we'll be in trouble.

Outside the horse, the Greek camp burst into activity. Following Odysseus' orders, the rest of the Greeks rolled up tents and bedding, packed away furniture, food, and animals, and loaded their ships. Soon, the only signs of the long war were scraps of litter swirling on the wind-blown plain... and the giant wooden horse outlined against the sea.

One Greek was left behind, Sinon. He was to play an important role in tricking the Trojans. The Greek commander Agamemnon, brother of the wronged Menelaus, explained what he had to do.

Your job is to convince the Trojans that they must take the horse into the city. You know what to do when the time comes: light a beacon, and we'll return. Good luck.

The Greeks have gone! They've left something behind.

But the Greeks had not left at all. They had only sailed out of sight.

Thinking that ten years of suffering were over, the Trojans poured out of the city gates. King Priam headed straight for the giant horse on the beach.

By Zeus, it's a giant horse: maybe they left it behind because they couldn't get it on board.

Look at this mess!

The Trojans gathered around the wooden horse in amazement. Someone suggested making a hole to see what was inside. The priest, Laocoon was sure it was a deadly trick and wanted to burn the horse. But King Priam saw the message to Athena carved into the horse's flank.

Laocoon threw a spear at the horse's flank with such force that the horse shook when it was hit.

We'll be destroyed if we take it into our city. Burn it!

Thud!

Inside, the spear narrowly missed the head of Neoptolemus, son of Achilles, but he didn't move. Around him others were sick with fear.

The arguments about the horse were interrupted. Shepherds pushed through the crowd and threw a man onto the ground. It was Sinon, the Greek who had been left behind on the beach... he'd been taken prisoner. Little did the Trojans know that this was all part of the Greek plan.

Please protect me, King Priam. I knew terrible secrets about Odysseus, so he tried to kill me. But I managed to escape when they were packing up.

Priam set Sinon free – after he promised to explain why the Greeks had built the horse.

Oh, that thing! They upset Athena and wanted to make it up to her. They made the horse big so you couldn't get it through your gates. They thought if you got it into Troy, Athena would switch sides and help you win the war.

He's lying. I bet that trickster Odysseus told him to say all that.

In desperation, Laocoon prayed to the sea god Poseidon for his help. He wasn't going to get it. Suddenly, two giant sea serpents rose high above crashing waves and headed straight for Laocoon's twin boys.

Poseidon, guide us!

Daddy! Look out!

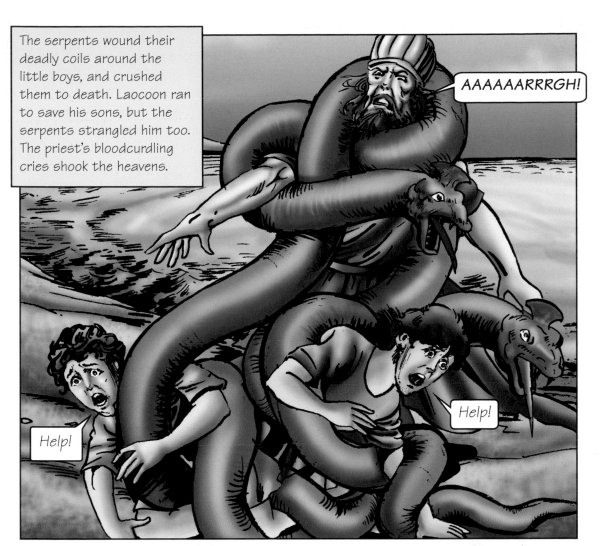

The serpents wound their deadly coils around the little boys, and crushed them to death. Laocoon ran to save his sons, but the serpents strangled him too. The priest's bloodcurdling cries shook the heavens.

AAAAAARRRGH!

Help!

Help!

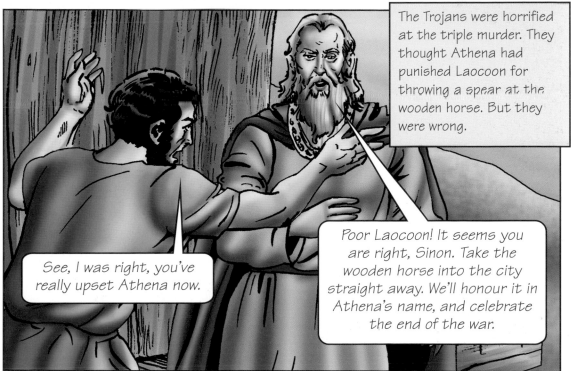

The Trojans were horrified at the triple murder. They thought Athena had punished Laocoon for throwing a spear at the wooden horse. But they were wrong.

See, I was right, you've really upset Athena now.

Poor Laocoon! It seems you are right, Sinon. Take the wooden horse into the city straight away. We'll honour it in Athena's name, and celebrate the end of the war.

The horse was huge and very heavy. But, the Trojan people put it onto a platform and placed logs underneath, to roll it along. They slung rough ropes around its neck, to pull it. Children and women followed, dancing, running and laughing. As the horse moved forward, no-one heard the clanking of the armour inside.

A couple of Trojans were still worried. One was the warrior Aeneas, son of a mortal man and the goddess Aphrodite. Aeneas was in charge of the Trojan forces. He stomped off to his camp on Mount Ida with a small band of his men.

King Priam's daughter, Cassandra could see into the future. She knew exactly what the Greeks were up to, but no-one listened to her warnings.

You fools. That horse is full of armed men!

What is she on about? Silly woman.

Finally, the horse was pulled to the city centre, and the festivities began. Sweet-scented roses were scattered around its feet. Golden daisies hung around the horse's neck. The townspeople danced and sang, and drank and feasted for the first time in ten long years. Inside the horse, the pick of the Greek armies sat, waiting for their moment.

Cheers! Praise to the goddess Athena!

Hurrah!

Athena had heard Helen praying that she wanted to go home. So she told Helen about her plan and offered to help her return home.

As soon as she could, Helen left the celebrations. She was excited at the thought of escaping from Troy.

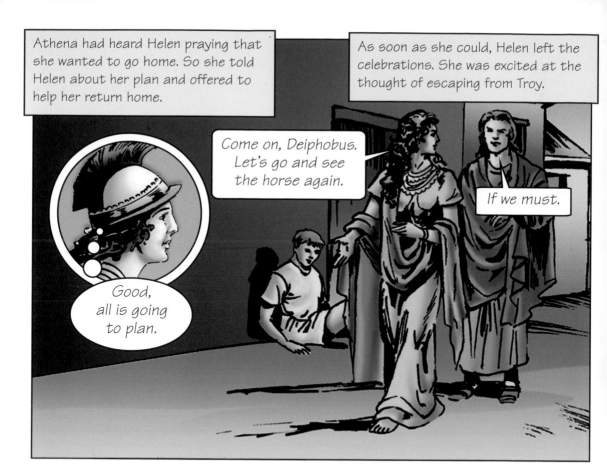

Come on, Deiphobus. Let's go and see the horse again.

If we must.

Good, all is going to plan.

Helen walked around the horse, smiling to herself. She tapped its hollow legs. Helen knew the warriors inside could hear her, and teased them by copying their wives' voices. Deiphobus thought she was being funny.

What a fine horse you are! I think I'll call you Odysseus, so long gone from me, your loving wife Penelope.

This is a silly game.

Inside the horse, the warriors were uncomfortable, nervous and bored. Neoptolemus jumped when he thought he heard his wife call his name, and nearly shouted out in reply. Odysseus silenced him just in time.

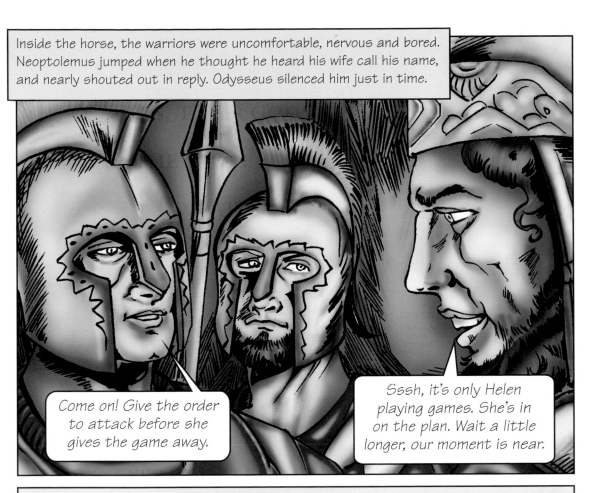

Come on! Give the order to attack before she gives the game away.

Sssh, it's only Helen playing games. She's in on the plan. Wait a little longer, our moment is near.

As night fell, Helen and Deiphobus walked back to the palace. The streets were quiet, apart from the sounds of snoring. The townspeople had returned to their homes, happy and tired from partying. A couple of sentries remained on guard. But they dropped off to sleep.

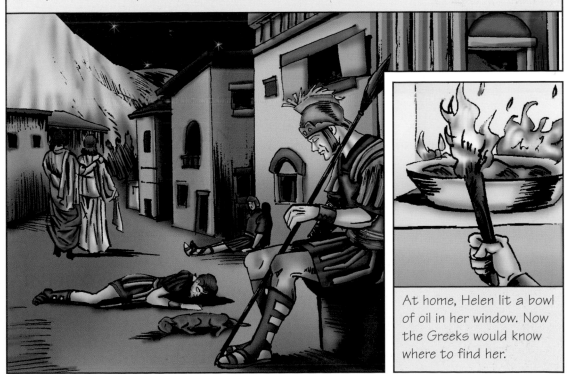

At home, Helen lit a bowl of oil in her window. Now the Greeks would know where to find her.

At midnight, a full moon rose over the sea.

In the shining path of moonlight on the sea, the Greek fleet waited.

The Trojans had forgotten about Sinon. He slipped away from where he had been watching the celebrations and headed for the city gates. He lifted the heavy bar, opened the gate and went out.

This is almost too easy!

The fleet should be able to see this roaring fire.

Sinon built a pile of driftwood and made a bright fire.

Sinon raced back to the city and headed straight for the wooden horse, dodging around the snoring sentries. He grabbed a rope, and pulled himself up to the trapdoor. Back on shore, the Greek ships had landed and hundreds of warriors were now advancing across the plain to the sleeping city.

Inside the horse, Epeius clicked open the secret trapdoor.

After their long wait, the Greek warriors were impatient. The first in line couldn't wait any longer, and jumped. But he'd forgotten how high the horse was and broke his neck when he landed.

Gasp!

Thud!

One by one, Greece's best soldiers dropped from their hiding place onto the silent city streets.

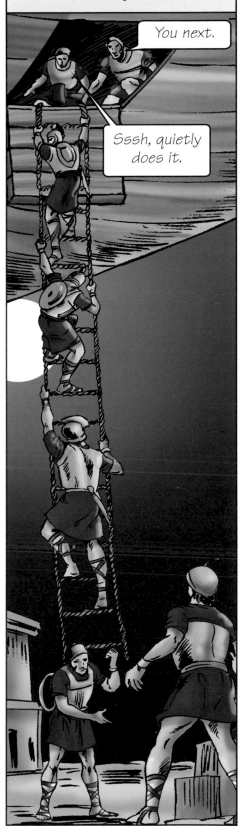

You next.

Sssh, quietly does it.

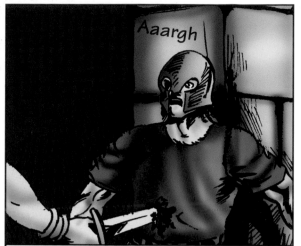

Their first job was to kill any sentries who might raise the alarm. The sentries were stabbed before they had time to wake up and realise what was happening.

One of Odysseus' men ran to open the city gates for the last time. The Greek armies were ready, the air around them tight with tension. At Agamemnon's command, they charged in, spears and swords drawn.

Charge! May Zeus give you courage!! Let Troy BURN!

The Greek soldiers burst into houses and cut the throats of men lying defenceless on their beds.

The Trojan commander, Aeneas rushed into the city from his camp on Mount Ida as soon as he heard the fighting. He saw the sleepy-eyed Trojans fighting desperately for their lives. Men were killed mercilessly, women and children dragged off and imprisoned.

They don't know what's hit them, or how. We don't stand a chance.

Aargh!

Aeneas and his men joined the fight. Greek soldiers were everywhere, running through houses and streets, uttering loud yells of triumph. In the smoke and flickering light of burning buildings, a group of Greek soldiers called to Aeneas and his men, mistaking them for fellow Greeks. They realised their mistake too late, and were murdered by the Trojans. The Greeks' mistake gave one of Aeneas' soldiers an idea.

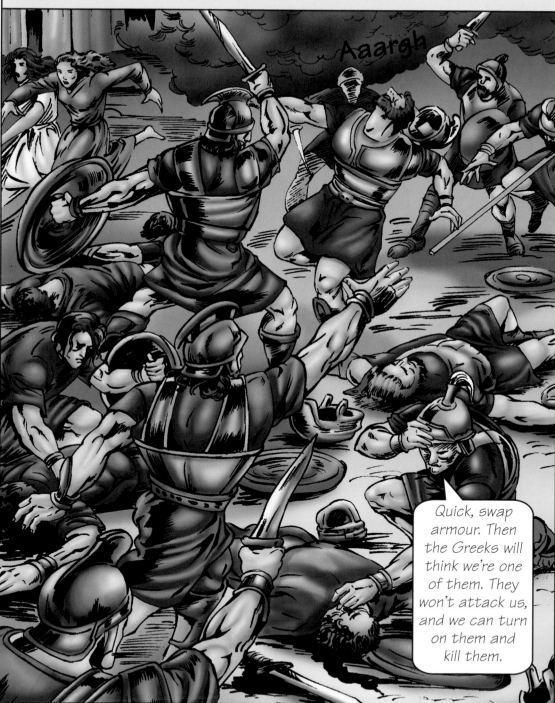

Quick, swap armour. Then the Greeks will think we're one of them. They won't attack us, and we can turn on them and kill them.

Aeneas and his men ran through the streets. They won many bloody fights. It was the only time in that long night that the Trojans had the Greeks running for their lives. Some Greeks ran back to their ships, others scrambled back up into the belly of the wooden horse.

Aeneas and his soldiers saw Priam's daughter, Cassandra, being dragged from a temple. Their disguise now turned against them. The Trojans on the temple roof fired lots of deadly arrows at them.

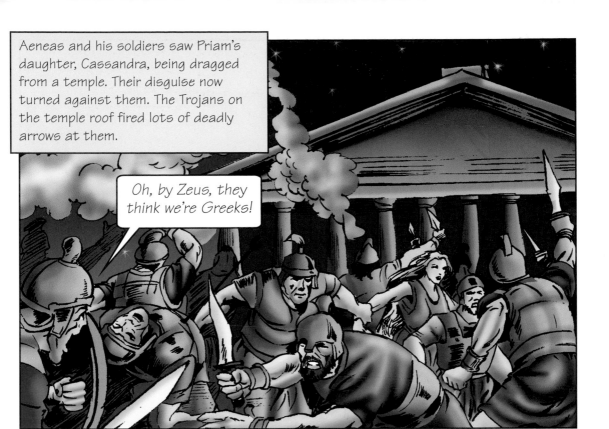

Oh, by Zeus, they think we're Greeks!

Poseidon sat on a mountain and watched the battle.

Even worse, the Greeks heard the foreign accents of Aeneas and his men and turned on them too. The brave Trojan soldiers were outnumbered. All, apart from Aeneas, were killed.

All is going to plan, as decided by the gods'.

They're not Greeks, get 'em!

Elsewhere, the Trojans had run out of weapons. They were tearing up roof tiles and breaking statues to use as missiles. But the streets were full of Greeks, their swords and spears flashing amongst the burning buildings.

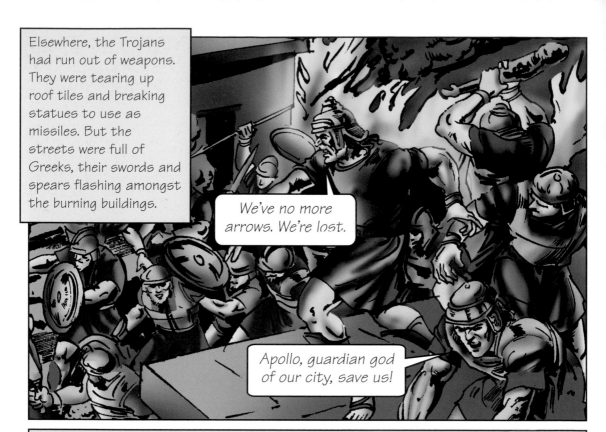

We've no more arrows. We're lost.

Apollo, guardian god of our city, save us!

King Priam's wife, Queen Hecuba fled to a safe place by the palace. There, beneath an ancient laurel tree, she gathered her daughters around her. King Priam put on the armour he hadn't worn for years, but it didn't hang well on his old, wasted body.

Stay with us, old man, you're too weak to fight.

Maybe you're right. What can my old bones do?

Suddenly, there was a clash of metal and shouting. The royal couple watched in horror as their son ran towards them. He was followed by the Greek hero Neoptolemus, who stabbed him. Their son's blood gushed out over the altar steps. Priam threw his spear at Neoptolemus, but his throw was weak. The spearhead bounced off Neoptolemus' shield.

Neoptolemus grabbed Priam and pulled him to the edge of the sanctuary. The old king's last sight, before Neoptolemus pushed his blade deep into the old man's body, was the blazing ruin of his city.

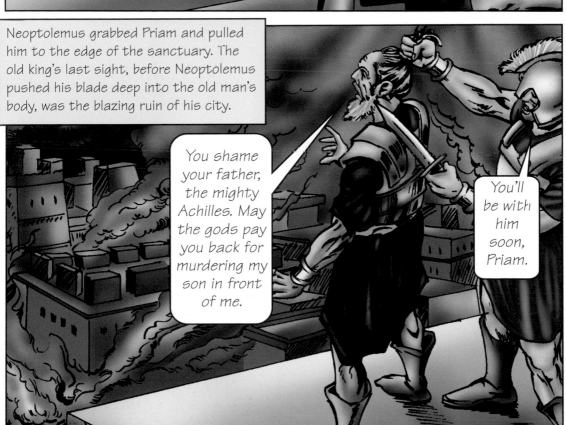

In the meantime, Aeneas stumbled home, along the ruined city streets. He saw Helen watching him from the palace, and was filled with hatred and anger. But his mother, Aphrodite spoke to him.

You! You are the curse of Troy. All this bloodshed, this terrible war… it's all your fault. You deserve to die. I will enjoy killing you.

My son, stay your sword. Don't waste your anger on this woman. Go to your father, your wife and your little son, and save them. It is not Helen's fault. It is the warring gods who are to blame.

Shown the way by Aphrodite, Aeneas made his way safely through the streets. On the way, she pointed out to him the work of the gods: the columns destroyed by Poseidon's earthquakes; the storm clouds gathered by Athena; Hera encouraging the Greek troops with battle cries. As Aphrodite promised, his family was unharmed, his home untouched, while everything around blazed.

Come, we must escape.

What's the point of living now that Troy is dead? I'm an old man, I'd rather die here, fighting to the last.

What! Run away? We should stand proud and defend our home to the last.

Just then, Aeneas' little boy's hair lit up as if with flames. It was a sign from the gods. On seeing it, Aeneas' family finally agreed to go with him.

While the battle continued, all Menelaus wanted to do was to see Helen. He took Odysseus with him, as Helen was bound to be closely guarded. High up, in the heart of the city, they saw a circle of light burning in a palace window. It was the fire that Helen had lit.

I'm going to kill that backstabbing woman. She made a fool out of me. And broke my heart.

Come on, this way. That window is where Helen is, the one with the light.

I think it's about time Helen lent a hand.

Helen was being guarded by her husband, Deiphobus and other Trojan warriors. Out of all the fights that day, this was the most terrible, caused by love, hatred, and revenge. Helen watched and waited.

Suddenly, Helen seized a dagger from a fallen soldier and stabbed it into the back of her husband, Deiphobus.

AAARGH...BETRAYER!

Menelaus couldn't believe his eyes. Helen had set herself free from blame. All thoughts of revenge drained from him as he was once more charmed by Helen's spirit and beauty. Menelaus threw down his sword.

Husband...forgive me... Will you take me home with you, where I belong?

Zeus, what a woman! Helen...

So, after 10 years of war and the countless deaths of brave men; after being embarrassed by Paris and an unfaithful wife, Menelaus forgave Helen. In love once more, he led her gently to his ship. Helen was going home.

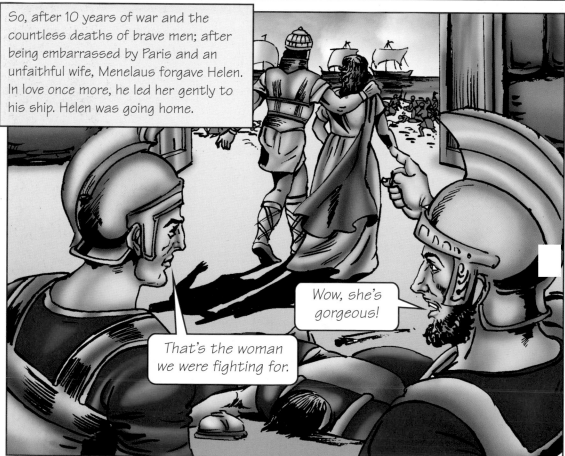

Wow, she's gorgeous!

That's the woman we were fighting for.

The battle was won, the last Trojans defeated and removed from the palace. The Greeks gathered a pile of treasure from the city: solid gold bowls and fine pottery, holy statues and beautifully made clothes. A Greek soldier guarded the long file of weeping women and children, taken to be slaves in Greece. Their husbands and fathers had all been killed.

The proud and ancient city of Troy was no more. Athena and Hera had their revenge, for Paris' rejection of them at that beauty contest so long ago.

Now, it was time to even things out. The same gods who helped the Greeks win the Trojan War would make them suffer. It was the price they had to pay for victory. The Greek king, Agamemnon, was the first one to suffer. He took King Priam's daughter, Cassandra as his wife. But when he returned home his first wife, Clytemnestra, wasn't pleased. She murdered Agamemnon in his bath.

Odysseus got the old queen, Hecuba, as a slave.

Odysseus also suffered. The gods made his return home very difficult. But that's another story…

As for the Trojans, all was not lost. Aeneas led the remains of the Trojan people through secret paths and tunnels beneath the city to Mount Ida. Once the Greeks finally left, they built a fleet of 20 ships. Apollo guided them to the east coast of Italy, where they built a new Troy.

We'll find a new home and rebuild Troy. It will be a great city again.

45

Beacon: *A fire lit as a signal.*

Brazier: *A heater on a stand that you can light a fire in.*

Fatally: *Leading to death or disaster.*

Fate: *Your destiny, the future course of your life, decided upon in advance by some supernatural force.*

Guardian god: *A god that is chosen or believed to have a special responsibility for protecting a place or a person.*

City-state: *It could be little more than a village and surrounding lands, or a big powerful fortified city such as Mycenae. A city-state had a centre of population with its own leader, laws and government.*

Demi-god: *A person who has both a human and a god parent. They usually have special powers inherited from the parent who is a god.*

Empire: *A group of states rules by a single king or queen.*

Immortal: *Living forever, with no death. The gods are immortal.*

Mortal: *Having a life that is ended by death, usually referring to humans as distinct from immortal gods.*

Myths: *The stories of a tribe or people that tell of their gods, heroes and turning points in their history.*

Offering: *A gift made to a god, such as a specially killed animal, as a thank you, or in the hope of winning the god's support.*

Olympian gods: *The top twelve gods whom the ancient Greeks believed ruled their lives, and whose home was Mount Olympus in northern Greece.*

Oracle: *A holy place or person in that place. People went there to ask advice about what to do, or what might happen to them in the future.*

Plunder: *To steal or take by force goods from people who have been conquered.*

Priest/priestess: *A man or woman who devotes his or her life to serving a god or goddesses.*

Revenge: *Getting your own back on someone who has harmed you, or for someone you care about.*

Sack: *To attack, destroy and plunder a city or building.*

Sanctuary: *A holy place, a building or an area of land where a god is worshipped and offerings may be made.*

Seer: *Someone who has visions of what will happen in the future.*

Sentry: *A soldier who is keeping guard over a certain place.*

Siege: *When an attacking army surrounds the enemy settlement or camp and prevents any supplies of food or water entering in. Those under siege starve to death or must surrender.*

Skirmish: *Irregular fighting, especially between small groups of soldiers.*

Superhuman: *Being stronger and smarter than a normal human.*

Trade route: *A path along which people stop and buy, or sell, goods. This can be on land, or at sea. Whoever controls a trade route can make a lot of money.*

Tribute: *A payment demanded by one city-state or country from another. It can be a punishment or a way for a powerful state to exert its power, and make money from a weaker one.*

Vain: *When somebody is very proud of their looks and skills.*

INDEX